D0504466

EX LIBRIS

VINTAGE CLASSICS

The Little Prince

ANTOINE DE SAINT-EXUPÉRY

The Little Prince

WITH ILLUSTRATIONS BY THE AUTHOR

TRANSLATED FROM THE FRENCH BY
Michael Morpurgo

VINTAGE

2 4 6 8 10 9 7 5 3 1

Vintage
20 Vauxhall Bridge Road,
London SW1V 2SA

Vintage Classics is part of the Penguin Random House group of companies
whose addresses can be found at global.penguinrandomhouse.com.

Penguin
Random House
UK

Translation copyright © Michael Morpurgo 2018

Michael Morpurgo has asserted his right to be identified as the translator of this
Work in accordance with the Copyright,
Designs and Patents Act 1988

First published in the US in 1943 by Reynal & Hitchcock, New York
First published in Great Britain in 1945 by William Heinemann

www.vintage-books.co.uk

A CIP catalogue record for this book is available from the
British Library

ISBN 9781784874179

Typeset in 12/15 pt Fournier MT
by Integra Software Services Pvt. Ltd, Pondicherry

Printed and bound in Italy by L.e.g.o. SpA

Penguin Random House is committed to a sustainable future for our
business, our readers and our planet. This book is made from
Forest Stewardship Council® certified paper.

Foreword

I wondered, as I was translating Antoine de St Exupéry's glorious book, whether there is any book in the English language that is as familiar to so many of us, as universally beloved, as frequently studied, as deeply revered, as *The Little Prince* is to the French. Unquestionably, we have many great and iconic books written in the English language that are widely read and loved and admired. But I can think of no single book of ours that appeals so widely across the generations, that remains so relevant, whose glow does not fade with the passing of time, that belongs as uniquely and particularly to the intellect and culture of its country of origin.

My conclusion, as I was working on this – as I tried to write in his voice, live inside the landscape of his imagination, to tell it as he heard it and saw it and meant it, but in my way and in English – is that it might be impossible to understand France and the French properly, unless you have read and known and loved this book.

Certainly I have discovered in translating it, that the best way to come to know a book intimately is to come to know the mind of the writer. I understand, and appreciate more fully now, the mastery of St Exupery's art and craft, the inspired brushstrokes of his storytelling. Translating this was a master class for me.

Some will not be surprised to know, after reading my translation of *The Little Prince*, that this was my first attempt at any kind of translation, probably since trying to translate pages of Racine's *Phèdre* when I studied French at school. I was no scholar then, when it came to French language or literature, and I am no scholar now.

I am however a maker of stories, a teller of tales. I have lived and breathed stories since I was a child. So to be asked to translate one of the greatest stories ever written was an honour I could not refuse. And if I am honest, I thought my knowledge of French would be just about up to it. Well, I was wrong about that.

The economy of St Exupéry's elegant yet complex prose – or is it poetry? – proved to be a real challenge to my rather limited and literal understanding of French. I knew of course that I could crib off the established translations, but I also knew I must not, that I should not take even a peeky look at them, but rather translate as best I could, tell it down from Exupéry's French my way, into my English, and then perhaps, if I really needed to, have a peeky look later. So that's what I did.

I also wanted to do this translation because I knew that so many English-speaking people have not had the joy of reading *The Little Prince*. It is a different book, unlike any other, strange, French. And in translation, the language can be inhibiting. Compared to the book's immense popularity amongst French readers, it seems to resonate much less with us.

There might be many reasons for this. Broadly speaking, and especially in children's books, we seem to like stories that are above all exciting. As children we love adventures that make us long to discover what happens next, with characters with whom we can identify strongly.

The Little Prince has all that, but it is much more the story of a relationship, a story that asks the great questions of life and death, of the human predicament. It is deeply intellectual and philosophical, and therefore deeply troubling.

And it is not a book that can be conveniently pigeonholed. Is it a children's book? Well, I suppose that depends on the grown-up reading it. The Little Prince does not have a high opinion of the capacity of grown-ups to understand the world of the child. Sadly, far too many of them have 'put away childish things'.

Anyway, I thought a new translation might enable more readers – children and grown-up children – to discover this wonderful but different book. I hope it does.

Great books can change us. Having immersed myself so completely in this story, I am sure I will never be able to look up at the stars again without thinking of the Little Prince up there somewhere.

And I will look at a flower differently, at people differently, whether businessmen, lamplighters or kings. I will think of myself differently too, and try even harder to look after and cherish the child in me, for the child in each of us is the heart and soul in each of us.

And I will be quite sure to check my engine before I set off in my aeroplane on a flight over a desert!

Michael Morpurgo, 2018

To Léon Werth

I want to apologise to all you children for having dedicated this book to a grown-up. I have a proper reason: this grown-up is my best friend in the whole world. And there's a second reason also: this grown-up understands everything, even books for children. And there's even a third reason: this grown-up lives in France where he is hungry and cold. He really does need cheering up. But if all these reasons are not good enough – and they are not – then I should like to dedicate this book to the child that this grown-up once was. All grown-ups were once children. (But very few of them seem to remember that!) That's why I am changing my dedication.

To Léon Werth
When he was a little boy.

Chapter I

When I was six years old I had a book on rainforests called *True Stories from Wild Life*. In it there was an amazing drawing, of a snake swallowing an animal, whole! This is a copy, done by me, of that picture.

Here's what it said in the book: Boa constrictors swallow their prey completely whole, without chewing at all. Afterwards they can't even move, and in order to digest what they have eaten, they have to sleep for a whole six months.

I thought long and hard about all this, and managed to draw a picture of the snake, in colour pencils. It was my first ever drawing, my Drawing Number One. And it looked like this:

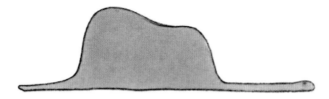

I showed my masterpiece to some grown-ups, and asked them if my drawing frightened them. They all said much the same thing: 'Why should a picture of a hat frighten us?'

But my drawing was not of a hat. It was of a boa constrictor who had eaten an elephant – so I then drew a picture of how the insides of such a boa constrictor might look, so that the grown-ups might understand. Grown-ups always need things explained to them. My Drawing Number Two looked like this:

The grown-ups told me I should not waste my time doing any more drawings of boa constrictors – whether of their insides or outsides – but in future concentrate more on geography, or history, or on mathematics or grammar. I was so upset at this response to my Drawing Number One and my Drawing Number Two, that I abandoned then, at the age of six, any hopes I might have had of becoming a great painter. Grown-ups seem to understand nothing for themselves. It is very boring for children always to have to explain things to them.

So, since I could not be an artist, I had to choose another profession. I took up flying. I became an aeroplane pilot. I have flown just about all over the world. So, it is true, my geography has been very useful. With just a glance I can always recognise where I am, I can easily tell the difference between China and Arizona. And this is very helpful, I find, when I am up there, flying through the night, and not at all sure of where I am.

In my lifetime of flying round the world, I have met lots of interesting people. I have lived most of my life amongst grown-ups, and had the chance to get to know them. I have to say this experience has not greatly improved my opinion of them.

When I do meet one of these grown-ups who seems a little more enlightened, I make it my business to try out on them a little experiment:

I show them my Drawing Number One, and my Drawing Number Two, which I have still kept until this time. I do this just to see how much they really understand. And always, without fail, they say: 'It's a hat'. So then I don't bother to talk to them about boa constrictors, nor rainforests, nor stars. I talk about what I know they are interested in: bridge, golf, politics and ties. They know they are talking to the right kind of person and they are happy.

Chapter II

So it was that I lived much of my life on my own, with almost no one to speak to. That is, until six years ago, when I was forced to crash-land my plane in the Sahara Desert. Something had gone wrong with my engine. I had no mechanic with me, and no passengers. I was alone. Somehow I had to find some way of repairing my engine. It was a question of life or death. I had only enough water left for eight days.

That first night I lay down to sleep on the desert sand knowing I was thousands of miles from the nearest living person. I was even more alone than a shipwrecked sailor lying on a raft in the middle of the wide, wide ocean. Imagine my surprise then when I was woken at dawn by a strange small voice.

''Scuse me,' the voice said, 'but I was wondering if you could draw me a sheep, please?'

'What?'

'A sheep. I want you to draw me a sheep.'

I leapt to my feet, as if I had been struck by lightning. I rubbed my eyes to be quite sure they were not deceiving me. No, I had seen what I had seen. An extraordinary looking little fellow was standing there scrutinising me intently.

This is the best portrait I did of him, a while later. But my drawing, it has to be said, is not nearly as good or as beautiful as he was in real life. That's not my fault though. If you remember, when I was six, I had been rather put off following my intended career as a painter by discouraging grown-ups. After that sad experience I had never really learnt to draw anything else, except boa constrictors, the insides and outsides of boa constrictors.

So anyway, I stood there, looking at this amazing and incongruous apparition, wide-eyed with wonder, as you can imagine. You must not forget that I was thousands of miles from any human habitation. And yet, this little fellow did not seem lost at all. He wasn't dying of exhaustion, or hunger or thirst. And he did not look frightened in the least. He just did not look like a lost child in the middle of the desert, a thousand miles from anywhere.

'What on earth are you doing here?' I asked him, when at last I had got over my surprise and found my voice.

But he simply repeated his strange request, very softly, very sweetly, and in complete seriousness. ''Scuse me, but I was wondering if you could draw me a sheep please?'

This whole situation, what he was asking me, was so utterly absurd that somehow I could not say no. I knew that it was equally absurd, a thousand miles from anywhere and anyone, and in serious danger of dying out there in the desert, to be taking a piece of paper and a pen out of my pocket. I told this little fellow, rather impatiently I fear, that my studies had included geography, history, mathematics and grammar, but not drawing, that I really was not much good at drawing.

'That does not matter,' he said. 'Don't worry about that. Just draw me a sheep.'

So, because I had never drawn a sheep, I did instead one of the only two drawings that I knew I could do, one of my boa constrictor drawings – the one with the swallowed elephant inside. I was amazed at his reaction.

9

'No, no!' he cried. 'I didn't want a drawing of an elephant inside a boa constrictor. A boa constrictor is very dangerous, and as for an elephant, it is huge, and would always get in the way. At home, where I come from, everything is small. I need a sheep. Draw me a sheep.'

So I drew him a sheep. He took one look at it. Then he said, 'No. That's no good at all. It looks already rather poorly to me. Do me another.'

So I did. My young friend smiled, but rather patronisingly, I thought.

'I'm afraid to have to tell you that this is not a sheep. It is a ram. It has horns.'

I did the drawing again, but he rejected it just as he had before.

'That one is too old. I want a sheep who will live for a long time.'

By now I had had enough of all this. I had no more time to waste. My engine needed stripping down. I had to get on with it. So very quickly I sketched this drawing, and showed it to him. 'There you are,' I told him. 'This is his box. The sheep you want is inside it.'

I was of course expecting another rejection. So you can imagine my surprise when I saw that his eyes were bright with enthusiasm.

'That's just what I wanted. Do you think a sheep like this will need a lot of grass?'

'Why do you ask?'

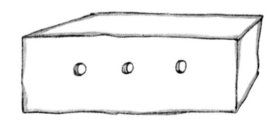

'Because as I told you where I live everything is rather small, and there's not much room to grow a lot of grass.'

'It'll be fine,' I told the little fellow. 'I have drawn you a tiny tiny little sheep.'

He leant forward and looked closely at the drawing now. 'Not so tiny as all that …' he said. 'Would you believe it! The sheep, he's fallen asleep.'

And that was how I first got to know the little prince.

Chapter III

It took me a while to find out where he had come from. The little prince would ask me question after question, but whenever I asked him anything, he never seemed to hear me. It was only from chance remarks he made that little by little I was able to discover anything at all about him.

But his questions just kept coming. So for instance, when he first set eyes on my aeroplane (and I shan't draw my aeroplane for you because it would be far too difficult) he immediately asked this question:

'What's that thing over there?'

'It's not a thing,' I told him. 'It flies. It's an aeroplane. It's my aeroplane.' I said this because it was important to me that he understood that I flew it, that I was a pilot and proud of it.

11

'What!' he cried. 'You just fell out of the sky?'

'I did,' I replied modestly, not wanting to make too much of it.

'Oh, that's funny,' he laughed. 'Really funny.'

The little prince had a merry sort of a laugh, one that pealed like bells, and one, which I have to say, irritated me greatly. I mean, my plane had just crashed. I wanted my misfortune to be taken rather more seriously. Then he went on: 'So, like me, you came down from up in the sky as well. Which planet are you from then?'

And that was when I began to understand something at last about where this mysterious little fellow might have come from.

'So you're from another planet too, are you?' I asked him.

But he didn't answer me. I saw he was shaking his head. He could not take his eyes off my aeroplane. 'I can't imagine' he said, 'that in that thing of yours over there, you could have travelled from very far away.'

He said no more for a while, but seemed to be lost in his own thoughts.

Then he took my sheep out of his pocket. I could see it had become like a precious treasure to him. He simply gazed down at it in wonder for several minutes.

You can imagine maybe how much I was intrigued by his strange reluctance to give me a straight answer as to which planet he came from. I had to try again, to know more.

'Where do you come from, young fellow?' I asked him. 'I mean, where's home? Where will you take my sheep to?'

There was a long and thoughtful silence. Then he said: 'What's really good about the box you have given me, is that it will now be a place he can go to at night times. It will be like a house for him.'

'That's a good idea,' I told him. 'And if you are good I can give you some string as well, and a post for you to tie him up to.'

But that idea really seemed to upset him.

'Tie him up? Why should I want to do that? What a strange idea.'

'Because if you don't,' I said, 'then he could wander off anywhere and get himself lost.'

The Little Prince on Asteroid B-612.

13

Then came that peal of laughter again. 'But where do you think he would go?' he asked.

'I don't know. Wherever he feels like. Straight ahead if he wants to.'

The little prince was suddenly serious. 'Well, that wouldn't be a very good idea. Everything is very small where I live.' Then he added, rather sadly: 'So straight ahead wouldn't get him very far.'

Chapter IV

So now I had discovered something else very important about the little prince: that the planet he came from was scarcely bigger than a house.

That in itself did not surprise me too much. I already knew that besides the great planets like Earth, Jupiter, Mars and Venus, which all had proper names, there were hundreds of others so small you could hardly see them through a telescope. I knew that when an astronomer

discovers one of these, he gives it only a number, rather than a name. So, for instance, he might call it: 'Asteroid-325'.

I have good reason to believe that this planet, from which the little prince had come, was 'Asteroid B-612'. This asteroid has only been seen once, through a telescope, by a Turkish

astronomer in 1909. He made a great announcement about his discovery in a lecture at The International Congress of Astronomy. But no one believed him, because of the clothes he was wearing. Grown-ups are like that.

Luckily for the good reputation of Asteroid B-612, a Turkish dictator made it a law which had to be observed, on pain of death, that everyone had to dress in the European style. The astronomer repeated his lecture in 1920, dressed in a suit that was thought to be supremely elegant. And this time they believed everything he said.

I have told you all this about Asteroid B-612, and its number too, mostly because of grown-ups. Grown-ups are very fond of numbers. When you tell them about a new friend, they never ask you the kind of questions that should be asked, such as: 'What kind of voice does he have?' 'What are his favourite games?' 'Does he collect butterflies?' Instead they ask: 'How old is he? How many brothers has he got? How much does he weigh? How much money does his father earn?' They really do imagine this is the best way to discover what sort of person he is!

If you tell grown-ups: 'I once saw a beautiful house built of pink bricks, with geraniums in the window box, and with doves on the roof,' they wouldn't be able to picture what this house was like at all. No, you have to tell them 'I once saw a

15

house that must have cost 100,000 francs.' Then they would exclaim: 'What a lovely house that must be!'

It would be the same if you told them: 'The proof of the existence of the little prince is that he was a beautiful person, that he laughed, and that he wanted a sheep. If anyone wants a sheep, that's proof enough that he exists.' Tell them that, and they would shrug their shoulders, and treat you like a child. But tell them that he comes from Asteroid B-612, and they will believe you at once, and they will not pester you any more with their stupid questions. They are like that. You mustn't hold it against them. Children have to remember always to be very tolerant towards grown-ups.

But those of us who understand life, we couldn't care less about silly old numbers. I should have liked to have begun this story as all fairy stories begin. I should like to have said: 'Once upon a time there was a little prince who lived on a planet scarcely bigger than he was, and who was longing to have a friend ... ' For those of us who understand how life really is, we know that would have been a far better way to begin, more believable.

But I wouldn't want anyone to skip too lightly through my book. It has not been at all easy for me, and sadder than you know, to write of these memories. It has already been six years since my friend went away with his sheep and left me. I tell you about him because I don't want to forget him. It is very sad to forget a friend. Not everyone has had a friend. And if I forget him, I could become like those grown-ups who are only interested in numbers.

That is why I bought a paintbox and pencils. It is really hard to try my hand at drawing again, now, at my age. Not since the age of six have I have ever attempted, until now, to draw anything, except the insides and outsides of a boa constrictor.

I will try my best, to draw as well as I can, to make the portraits as lifelike as possible. But I can never be sure things will work out quite as I intend. One drawing may look fine, the next one not. I do get size and proportion wrong too. In one picture the little prince is too big, in the next too small. I know the colour of his clothing might not look right either. I try a little more of this and a little less of that, and just hope it comes out all right. I know I do make certain mistakes with details that are really important. For that, I am truly sorry. My friend never explained things properly at all. Maybe he thought he did not need to, that I was more like him than I really am. The trouble was that I never could see sheep through boxes as he could. Perhaps I'm a little like a grown-up. Maybe I have grown old already.

Chapter V

Every day I learnt something new about his planet, about how he had left it, and the journey he had undertaken. All this information came in dribs and drabs, by chance, as thoughts came to him. This was how, on the third day after we met, I heard about the terrible baobab saga.

This time again it was all because of the sheep, in a way. The little prince seemed suddenly overwhelmed by some dreadful anxiety.

'Are you sure that sheep do eat little bushes?'

'Yes,' I told him. 'Quite sure.'

'Good. I'm happy then.'

I did not understand at all why it was so important to him that a sheep should eat little bushes. But then, still rather worried, he added: 'So they must also eat baobabs?'

I then had to tell the little prince that baobabs were not little bushes, that they were huge trees, as tall as a church tower, and that even if he took with him an entire herd of elephants, they would not manage between them to eat up a single baobab.

The idea of a troop of elephants clearly amused the little prince.

'You'd have to stand them one on top of the other,' he laughed.

But then, more thoughtfully, he said: 'Baobabs, you know, before they grow big, always begin by being small.'

'Of course. But I don't quite understand why you should want your sheep to eat baobabs when they are small?'

'Really? You don't know?' he said, as if it was obvious. I tried very hard to work it out for myself, and it was not at all easy. Anyway, it seems that on the little prince's planet, as on all planets, there were good plants and bad plants, and so of course there were good seeds from the good plants, and bad seeds from the bad plants. But seeds are invisible. They lie dormant hidden deep in the dark of the earth until one of them has the notion it would be a good idea to wake up. This little seed will first have a stretch, then grow slowly, ever so slowly, up towards the sunlight, until at last there it is, a sweet little innocuous twig of a plant. If it is the first shoot on a radish perhaps, or the early sprig of a rose, then it can be left to grow on as it wishes. But if this is a bad plant, you should pull it up at once, the moment you recognise it for what it is.

Now, there were some terrible seeds hiding away in the earth on the planet of the little prince, and these were the seeds of the baobab tree. All over the planet the soil was infested with them. And with a baobab, if you don't deal with it at once, if you leave it too late you will never ever be able to get rid of it. It will take over the entire planet, perforate it with the roots. And if the planet is too small, which it is, and if there are too many baobabs, they will overwhelm, and destroy the planet, and that would be that.

'It's just a question of self discipline,' the little prince explained later. 'First thing in the morning you look after yourself, you brush your teeth and wash your face, don't you? Well, the second thing you must do is to look after the planet. You pull up all the little baobabs, just as soon as you can tell the difference between them and the little rose bushes which can look a lot like them when they are very young. It's easy enough work, even if it is rather boring.'

And then one day he said to me: 'I think you ought to make a beautiful drawing for the children where you come from, so they can understand all about this. If ever they were to go off on their travels, it might prove very useful to them. There's sometimes no harm in putting off till tomorrow what should be done today, but when it comes to baobabs, any delay at all is always disastrous. I once knew of a planet where there lived the laziest man you could ever imagine. He just couldn't be bothered to dig up three little baobab bushes. It did not end well for him, nor his planet.'

So just as the little prince had asked, I made a drawing of that planet. I don't like to be didactic or moralistic, but I could see the dangers posed by baobabs are hardly known, and anyway the risks taken by anyone venturing into an asteroid are so dangerous that I decided, just for once, that I should set aside my usual inclinations, and tell it loud and clear.

'Children! Look out for baobabs!'

I worked so hard on this drawing in order to warn my friends of the grave danger they had been facing for so long, and like myself, without even knowing it. I had to tell them, to warn them.

You might well be wondering why there aren't any more big drawings of baobab trees like this in the book. Well, the answer is simple enough. I did try, but I just couldn't do another one. I think I could only draw a baobab tree when I needed to, when it really mattered. Baobab trees are a serious matter.

The Baobabs.

Chapter VI

Dear little prince, it took me a while to begin to understand just how sad
your little life must have been. For so long, all you had for enjoyment
was the beauty of sunsets. I only learnt about this on the morning of the
fourth day, when you said to me:

'I love sunsets. Come on, let's go and see one, right now.'

'But we can't. We have to wait.'

'Wait? Wait for what??'

'Until the sun goes down. We have to wait until it is time.'

You looked very surprised at that, and then you began laughing,
laughing at yourself.

'Oh, silly me,' you said. 'I was thinking I was still back home.'

Of course, as we all know, when it is midday in America, the sun is
going down in France. So you'd have to be able to get to France in one
minute flat, in order to witness the same sunset. France is a very long
way away, so it's just not possible. But on your tiny planet, my dear little

prince, I suppose all you would have to do is move your chair just a little and you could see dawn and dusk any time you want to.

'One day,' you told me, 'I watched the sun set forty-three times …' And then later, you went on: 'When I'm feeling really sad, I love to see a sunset.'

'So,' I asked him, 'on that day when you saw forty-three sunsets, were you still sad?'

But the little prince said nothing.

Chapter VII

On the fifth day – and again, this was thanks to the sheep – the little prince let slip more about himself. He came out suddenly with it, and with no warning, as if he had been churning it all over in his mind for a long time.

'A sheep, does it also eat flowers as well as little bushes?'

'A sheep,' I told him, 'eats just about everything it comes across.'

'Even flowers that have thorns?'

'Certainly. Even flowers with thorns.'

'And when it comes to thorns,' he went on, 'what are they for?'

I didn't know. At that particular moment I was very busy, trying to unscrew a nut in my engine that just would not budge. I was very worried by now, because the breakdown was beginning to look more and more serious. Worse still, my drinking water was running out.

'Thorns,' he said, 'what are they for, exactly?'

Once he had asked a question, the little prince would never give up until he had an answer. I was still struggling with my wretched nut, which seemed to be stuck fast, so I told him the first thing that came into my head. 'Thorns are no use for anything much. If you ask me, flowers only have thorns out of spite.'

'Oh, surely not,' he said, and then after a moment or two of hurt silence, went on: 'I can't believe that. Flowers are weak, and simple. Surely they are only protecting themselves as best they can. They just hope their thorns look terrifying, so that ...'

I said nothing. I wasn't listening. All I could think of at that moment was that if the nut refused to budge I was going to get my hammer and give it a good whack.

But once again, the little prince interrupted my thoughts, and would not let me get on. 'So you really believe, do you, that flowers ...'

I had had enough. 'No! No!' I shouted at him. 'I don't really believe anything. I just said the first thing that came into my head, that's all. I'm busy, can't you see? I have more important things to get on with.'

He was staring at me in utter amazement. 'What do you mean? More important things!' What must I have looked like, bent over this horrible old engine, hammer in hand, fingers covered with engine-grease. 'You sound just like a grown-up.' His words made me feel ashamed. And he hadn't finished with me yet.

'You confuse everything!' he went on, his golden hair blowing in the wind, 'you deliberately mix everything up!' He was really angry now.

'I once went to a planet where there lived a stiff-necked, red-faced old fool of a gentleman who never smelled a flower in his life. He never once looked up at a star. He never loved anyone. All he ever did in his entire life was add up numbers. All day long, like you did just now, he just kept on repeating over and over again: "I have more important things to be getting on with. I have more important things to be getting on with." And because of this he became puffed up with pride. In the end, he wasn't a man at all, he was a mushroom!'

'A what?'

'A mushroom!'

The little prince was so enraged by now that he had gone quite pale.

'For millions of years,' he went on, 'flowers have been growing thorns, and for millions of years, despite this, sheep have gone on eating flowers. Don't you think it worthwhile to try to understand why they should go to all that trouble to grow thorns if they don't serve a useful purpose? You don't think it's important, this age-old struggle for existence between sheep and flowers? Is it not a significant matter, more important than simply adding up numbers, like the stiff-necked, red-faced old fool of a gentlemen I met on that planet? Say I knew of a flower unique in the whole world, that grew nowhere else except on my planet, and that a little sheep might come along one morning and destroy it in one bite, just

like that, without realising that he was doing it, do you not think that is important?'

He went on, his face aglow now with passion.

'If someone loves a flower, unique in all the millions and millions of stars, and it makes him happy to look up there and remember his flower, isn't that enough in itself? He'll be thinking: "My flower is up there somewhere." But if a sheep comes along and she eats that flower, for him it would be as if all the starlight was put out! And you say, that's not important!'

He could not say any more. His words were drowned in tears. Night had fallen by this time. I dropped my tools. My hammer didn't matter any more, nor my nuts, nor even the prospect of dying of thirst. On this one star, this one planet, here, now, on my

25

own planet Earth, the little prince needed comforting. Nothing else mattered. I put my arms around him, and held him, rocking him gently.

'Dear little prince,' I began, 'the flower you love so much is no longer in danger. I will draw a muzzle for your sheep. I will draw railings to protect your flower … I will …'

Everything I tried to say sounded so maladroit, so clumsy. I did not know whether to try to stop him crying, or to join in and cry with him. How strange it is, this valley of tears.

Chapter VIII

I came to know quite quickly more about this little flower. There had always been these flowers on the little prince's planet, very simple small flowers, crowned with just one ring of petals. They took up very little room, and did not get in anyone's way. They would appear one morning in amongst the grass, and by nightfall would have faded away. But then, one day, from a seed blown in from who knows where, a new seedling had sprung up. The little prince had examined it closely and soon realised that it did not look like anything he had seen growing on his planet before. It could be, he thought, a new kind of baobab altogether.

This little seedling suddenly stopped growing and began to become a flower. The little prince was there to witness the appearance of a huge bud, and he knew already that this bud would grow something quite miraculous. This flower was not simply going to emerge from the shelter of its green bud, and be beautiful. She would hide away inside, choose her colours with the greatest care, clothe herself in her finery slowly, arranging her petals one by one. She did not wish to come out all crumpled like a poppy. She wanted to show herself to the world in the full glory of her beauty. Oh yes, she was quite a coquettish little flower. She took days and days to get herself ready. And then one morning, there she was, in full and splendid flower, at the very moment the sun rose. And this flower, who had worked so hard to make sure everything about her appearance was just perfect, could only yawn, and say: 'Oh, I am sorry, I've only just woken up. Look at me I'm such a mess, My petals are all bedraggled.'

The little prince could not contain his admiration for her: 'You are so beautiful,' he breathed.

'Aren't I just?' the little flower replied sweetly. 'And what's more, I was born at the very same moment as the sun.'

Although modest she most definitely was not, none the less this little flower touched his heart deeply. 'I think,' the flower went on, 'that it's just about time for my breakfast. Be so kind as to tend to my needs.'

And the little prince, rather taken aback at this, but wanting to do what he could to look after the little flower, went off at once to look for a watering can and some fresh water.

But it was not long before this rather haughty and demanding attitude became too much for the little prince to put up with. For example, one day, she was talking to the little prince about her four thorns, and said: 'Let tigers come. I'm not afraid of them, or their claws.'

'There aren't any tigers on my planet,' the little prince protested, 'and besides, tigers don't eat plants.'

'I am not a plant,' replied the flower.

'Well, excuse me … ' the little prince said.

'And anyway, I am not at all frightened of tigers. But I am terrified of draughts. I need something to protect me from the wind, a cloche maybe?'

The little prince was thinking: 'Terrified of draughts! That's bad luck if you are a plant. This is certainly a very complex sort of a flower.'

'In the night time,' the little flower went on, 'you had better make sure I am protected under a cloche. It's so cold here, on this planet of yours, not at all like mine. Now, where I come from ...'

But there she had to stop herself. After all she had come as a seed. There was no way she could ever have known other planets. Clearly embarrassed to have allowed herself to be caught out trying to make up such a silly story, she coughed two or three times, to make the little prince feel guilty.

'So what's keeping you?' she said, coughing again.' 'Where's this cloche then?'

'I was about to go, but you were still talking to me.'

Of course she was forcing herself to cough to make the little prince feel even more ashamed that he hadn't yet gone to fetch the cloche she had asked for.

So the little prince, despite his great affection for this little flower, was beginning to have his doubts about her. He had taken to heart all the ridiculous nonsense she was talking, and it made him feel very unhappy.

'I shouldn't have paid any attention to

her,' he told me one day. 'You should never listen to flowers. They are for looking at, for their scent. My own flower filled my whole planet with her fragrance, but none of this gave me any pleasure. This whole story of tigers and claws, which really had irritated me, should have filled my heart with tenderness and sympathy.

'I decided that before this I had understood nothing, about this little flower,' the little prince continued, 'that I should judge her, not by her words but by what

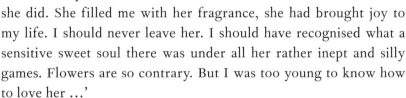

she did. She filled me with her fragrance, she had brought joy to my life. I should never leave her. I should have recognised what a sensitive sweet soul there was under all her rather inept and silly games. Flowers are so contrary. But I was too young to know how to love her …'

Chapter IX

When the little prince left his planet he was greatly helped, it seems, by a flock of migrating birds. On this morning of his departure he arranged everything just as it should be. He raked out both his two active volcanoes – these were especially useful for heating his breakfast every morning. He did have another volcano also, which was extinct. But, as

He raked out both his two active volcanoes.

he said. 'You never know!' So he also raked out that one too. If they are kept clean and tidy volcanoes burn away quite happily, and don't erupt. Volcanic eruptions are like chimney fires. Of course on planet Earth we are far too small to rake out our volcanoes, which is why they cause so many problems.

It was with some sadness that the little prince pulled up the last of the baobab shoots. He thought it likely he would never be back again, so every one of these little daily chores were very important to him that morning. As he was watering his dear little flower for the very last time and was about to lower the cloche over her, to shelter her, he found he was near to tears.

'Goodbye,' he said to the flower.

But she did not reply.

So he said it again: 'Goodbye.'

The flower coughed, but it wasn't because she had a cold.

'I was stupid and mean to you,' she told him. 'And I'm sorry. I want you to be happy.'

The little prince was amazed at this sudden change in her. He stood there quite bewildered, still holding the cloche over her. He just could not understand this new gentleness and thoughtfulness in her.

'I do love you, you know,' his flower told him. 'And it's all my fault you didn't understand that. Anyway, it doesn't really matter, not really, because when all's said and done, you were just as silly as I was. We must try to be happy, that's what I say. And you can put that cloche down now. I don't want it any more.'

'But what about the wind?'

'Oh, my cold sounds worse than it is. It's not so bad. The cool night air will do me good. I am a flower, after all.'

'But what about all those wild creatures out there?' said the little prince.

'Well, as I see it, if I ever want to see butterflies, I think I have to put up with two or three caterpillars, don't you? I hear butterflies are very beautiful. And if the butterflies and the caterpillars are not around, who else will come to see me? You are going to be far away on your travels, aren't you? And as for any wild animals, I'm not frightened of them, not one bit. I have my claws, remember.'

And to remind me, she showed me her four little thorns. Then she said: 'And what are you hanging around for anyway? It's really annoying me. If you are going, just go.'

She didn't want the little prince to see her crying. She was such a proud little flower.

Chapter X

The little prince was soon travelling in amongst the asteroid field, specifically to asteroid numbers 325, 326, 327, 328, 329 and 330. He wanted to visit each one of them to widen his knowledge and to discover all he could.

On the first asteroid there lived a king. Dressed in purple and ermine, he was seated on a throne that was both modest but also majestic at the same time.

'Oh, look!' cried the king on seeing the little prince. 'A subject!'

The little prince wondered how the king had recognised him when he had never seen him before. He did not realise that kings see the world in a rather simplistic way, that for them everyone is a subject.

'Come close, so that I can see you better,' said the king, who was delighted and proud to discover that at last he had found someone to rule over.

The little prince looked about him for somewhere he might sit down, but the whole planet was covered by the king's magnificent ermine cloak. So he just had to remain standing, and because he was rather tired by now, he yawned.

'It is against court etiquette to yawn in the presence of the King,' said the monarch. 'I absolutely forbid it!'

'I can't help it,' replied the little prince, who was rather bewildered. 'I have come a long way and haven't slept a wink.'

'Very well then,' the king said to him, 'then I order you to yawn. I haven't seen anyone yawning for years now. So the sight of yawning is very interesting for me and rather intriguing. So, yawn again! It is my command.'

'You've made me nervous ... I can't do it now,' said the little prince, who was covered in confusion by all this.

'Well, well ... ahem ...' the king said. 'Well then, I order you to ... to yawn ... sometimes ...' He was spluttering and was clearly vexed.

Of course the king expected his authority always to be respected. He would not tolerate disobedience of any kind. He was an absolute monarch. But, because he was a good sort of a man, he only gave orders that were reasonable and sensible.

For example, he might say: 'If I ordered a general to transform himself into a seabird, and the general did not obey me, then that wouldn't be the general's fault, would it? It would be my fault.'

'Might I sit down now, please?' the little prince ventured to ask.

'I order you to sit down,' the king told him, and most graciously he made available a fold of his ermine cloak for the little prince to sit on.

The more he thought about it, the more the little prince was astonished. The planet was tiny. What was there for this king to reign over?

'Sire,' he began, 'I beg you to excuse me for asking you a question, but ...'

The king interrupted him at once. 'I command you to ask me a question,' he said.

'Sire ... what exactly do you reign over in this place?'

'Everything,' replied the king. He said it with such majestic simplicity.

'Everything?'

With a sweep of his hand the king made the extent of his kingdom quite obvious: he was king of not only his planet, but all the other planets they could see, and the stars as well.

'Over all of that?' asked the little prince.

'All of it,' the king replied.

So this was not just an absolute monarch, but a universal monarch.

'And the stars obey you then?' asked the little prince.

'Of course they do,' said the king. 'They obey me instantly. I do not tolerate any indiscipline, I assure you.'

Such power amazed the little prince. If he had power like that he could watch the sunset not just forty-four times a day, but seventy-two, even a hundred or two hundred times in the same day, without ever having to move his chair! But then, because he was full of sadness at the sudden thought of his home, of the little planet he had abandoned, he was emboldened to ask a favour of the king:

'I should love to see a sunset,' he said. 'Do me the great kindness, please, sire, of commanding the sun to set for me.'

'If I were to command a general,' the king replied, 'to fly from one flower to another like a butterfly, or to write a great tragedy, or to change himself into a seabird, and if this general did not obey the order I had given him, who is to blame, the general or me?'

'It would be you,' the little prince told him: 'no question.'

'Precisely. You have to expect from everyone only what it is possible for them to do. All authority is based on reason. If you order your people to go and throw themselves in the sea, there would be a revolution. I have the right to expect them to obey me only if my orders are reasonable.'

'Yes, but what about my sunset?' asked the little prince again. Once he had asked a question, the little prince would never simply forget it – he insisted on an answer.

'You will have your sunset, I shall command it,' said the king. 'I'm just waiting for the conditions to be right before I give the order – that is part of my science of government.'

'And when will that be?' the little prince went on.

'Well well … ahem … let me see,' the king replied, consulting a huge calendar before he spoke again. 'Let me see, let me see. It will be … about … about … it will be about twenty minutes to eight. Then you shall see just how well I am always obeyed.'

The little prince yawned. He was disappointed he was not going to be able to get his sunset after all, and he was becoming somewhat bored too.

'Well, if there's nothing more for me here,' he said. 'I'm off!'

'Don't go,' replied the king, who was so proud and happy to have a subject at last. 'Don't go. I will make you a minister!'

'A minister of what?'

'Of … let me think … of Justice!'

'But there is no one around to judge.'

'We don't know that,' the king insisted. 'I haven't yet travelled the whole length and breadth of my kingdom. I am very old. There's no room for a carriage, and it would be far too exhausting to go on foot!'

'But I've already seen all there is to see of your kingdom,' said the little prince, turning to have another good look at the other side of the planet. 'And there's no one there.'

'Well in that case, you could judge yourself,' said the king. 'That's very hard indeed, you know, much more difficult than to judge others. It is a wise man who can judge himself.'

'I am quite capable of judging myself wherever I am,' said the little prince. 'I do not have to be here.'

'Well well … ahem …' the king began, 'somewhere on my planet I know there is an old rat. I hear him at night times. Say you judge the old rat. Say you condemn him to death from time to time. So his life depends on your sense of justice. You will have to spare his life, of course. There is only one of them on the planet, you see.'

The little prince replied: 'Actually, I don't approve of the death sentence. And now I really think I should be going.'

'No,' said the king.

The little prince, although he had said all he wanted to say, and done all he wanted to do on this planet, did not want to upset the old king.

'If Your Majesty likes to be obeyed upon command, at once, you could give me a reasonable command. You could, for instance, order me to be gone inside a minute. Conditions look favourable, I think, Your Majesty.'

The little prince waited a moment for a reply but the king didn't seem to have anything more to say.

With some sadness the little prince turned and walked away. As he was leaving, the king called out after him: 'I will make you my Ambassador,' he cried – he was still full of his majestic airs and graces.

On his way again the little prince thought to himself: 'These grown-ups are really odd.'

Chapter XI

On the second planet the little prince travelled to there lived a man who was extraordinarily conceited.

'Aha! A visit from one of my fans!' he cried, when he first saw the prince coming. For men such as this, everyone else was an admirer, a fan.

'Good morning, sir,' said the little prince. 'That's some hat you're wearing.'

'Very useful for welcoming my fans, for acknowledging their applause. But unfortunately no one ever comes here.'

'Really?' said the little prince, who did not quite understand.

'I'll show you. Clap your hands one against the other,' the man went on.

The little prince did as he was told and clapped his hands. The man responded by doffing his hat in acknowledgement of this applause.

'Well at least this is more fun than the visit to the King,' thought the little prince. So he went on clapping his hands, and of course the man went on

doffing his hat. But after five minutes of all this, the little prince did get fed up with the rather monotonous game.

'And what would I have to do,' the little prince asked him, ' to make the hat fall off?'

But the man was not listening. Such puffed-up people only ever listen to praise and flattery.

'I want you to tell me just how much you admire me,' said the man.

'What exactly do you mean by "admire"?' asked the little prince.

'To admire me,' replied the man, 'means to recognise that I am the most handsome man on the planet, the best dressed, the wealthiest, and the most intelligent.'

'But you are the only man on this planet,' the little prince told him.

'Admire me all the same,' said the man, 'just as a favour.'

The little prince shrugged, and said: 'All right then. I admire you. But I really don't understand why that should be so important to you.'

And the little prince went off. Once on his way again he kept thinking to himself : 'These grown-up folk are really very odd.'

Chapter XII

On the next planet the little prince came to on his travels there lived a man who was a drunk. This visit was over very quickly, and left the little prince feeling deeply depressed.

He found him sitting in silence surrounded by piles of bottles, some empty, some full. 'What are you doing here?' the little prince asked him.

'I'm drinking,' the drunk told him, gloomily.

'But why are you drinking?' the little prince asked him.

'To forget.'

'To forget what?' the little prince enquired, already feeling very sorry for this sad man.

'To forget that I am ashamed,' confessed the drunk, hanging his head in shame.

'Ashamed of what?' the little prince asked, wanting to help him somehow.

'I'm ashamed of drinking,' the drunk replied, and then lapsed into a deep silence.

Perplexed, the little prince went on his way, thinking all the while: 'My goodness, some of these grown-up folk are really very strange folk indeed.'

Chapter XIII

The fourth planet on the little prince's travels belonged to a businessman. This man was so wrapped up in his work that he did not so much as look up when the little prince arrived.

'Good morning,' the little prince said. 'Did you know your cigarette is out?'

'Three and two makes five. Five and seven makes twelve. Twelve and three makes fifteen. Good morning. Fifteen and seven makes twenty-two. Twenty-two and six, that's twenty-eight. No time to light it again. Twenty-six and five, equals thirty-one. Wow! That makes five hundred and one million, six hundred and twenty-two thousand, seven hundred and thirty-one.'

'Five hundred million what?' the little prince asked.

'What? You still there? Five hundred and one million … I forget … I have so much work on. This is work of the greatest importance. I don't have time for chitchat. Two and five equals seven … '

'Five hundred and one million of what?' the little prince repeated, who never in his life gave up once he had asked a question.

The businessman looked up. 'It's been fifty-four years that I've lived here on this planet,' he began. 'And I've only been disturbed three times. The first time was twenty-two years ago by a May bug that came from goodness only knows where. He kept making the most dreadful noise, as a result of which I made four mistakes in my calculations. The second time – eleven years ago now – it was an attack of rheumatism that interrupted my work. I don't do enough exercise, that's my trouble. But I don't have time to go messing about . I have work to get on with, work of the greatest importance. And the third time … is now! You! Now where was I? Oh, yes, I was up to five hundred and one million.'

'Five hundred and one million what?' asked the little prince.

The businessman understood by now that there would be no hope of peace and quiet until he answered the question.

'Millions of these little things you can sometimes see up in the sky.'

'You mean flies?'

'No, no. Little shiny things. You know.'

'Bees?'

'No, no. Little goldeny things that make lazy people daydream. But I have work to get on with, work of the greatest importance. I don't have time for daydreaming.'

'Oh, I know!' said the little prince. 'You mean stars!'

'That's it. Stars.'

'And what do you do with all these five hundred million stars?'

'Five hundred and one million, six hundred and twenty-two thousand, seven hundred and thirty-one. My work is of the greatest importance. I have to be precise.'

'And what do you do with these stars?'

'What do I do with them?'

'Yes.'

'Nothing. I just own them.'

'You own the stars!'

'Yes.'

'But I've just met with a king of one of these stars, who … '

'Kings own nothing. They rule, and that's very different.'

'But what good does it do you to own the stars? '

'It makes me rich.'

'But what's the good of being rich?'

'It means I can buy other stars, should anyone discover them.'

The little prince was thinking: 'This man is reasoning quite like the drunk on the other planet.' And on he went with his questions.

'How exactly can anyone own stars?'

'So who do you imagine they belong to anyway?' the businessman retorted, rather grumpily.

'I don't know. To no one, probably.'

'Exactly. So they belong to me, because I was the first to think of it.'

'And that's good enough reason, is it?'

'Of course it is. If you find a diamond that belongs to no one, then it's yours. If you discover an island that belongs to no one, then it's yours. When you are the first to invent an idea, you patent it, don't you? It's yours. I own the stars, for the simple reason that no one before me ever dreamed of owning them. Understand?'

'All right,' said the little prince. 'But if you own them, what can you do with them?'

'I manage them,' replied the businessman. 'I count them, and then count them again. It's difficult work, but it is work of the greatest importance.'

The little prince was still not satisfied. 'Listen,' he said. 'Say I own a silk scarf, I can wrap it around my neck, can't I? And say I own a flower, I can pick it, and take it with me, can't I? You can't pick up a star and take it with you, can you?'

'No, but I can put it in a bank,' replied the businessman.

'How do you mean?'

'It means that I can write down on a little piece of paper the number of stars I own, and then put that piece of paper away in a drawer and lock it up.'

'That's it?'

'That's all that's needed!'

The little prince was thinking: 'That may be quite an amusing idea, even poetic, but it doesn't make much sense.'

He clearly had rather different ideas from these grown-up folk about what made sense and what did not, about what was important and what was not.

'I myself happen to own a flower,' the little prince went on to tell him, 'that I water once a day. I own three volcanoes that I rake out once a week. (I even rake out the one that is extinct, because you never know.) But I don't just own my volcanoes, and my flower, I am useful to them. You may own your stars, but you do nothing for them.'

The businessman opened his mouth, but could say nothing in reply. The little prince decided this was a good moment to leave.

Once on his travels again, the little prince kept thinking: 'Grown-ups are really quite extraordinary.'

Chapter XIV

The fifth planet was altogether a very curious place. It was the smallest of them all. There was just about room on it for one street lamp and one lamplighter. The little prince could not work out what purpose they could possibly serve, up there in the sky, on this tiny planet that was without houses, without anyone there except the lamplighter.

'All right, so this lamplighter may seem ridiculous,' thought the little prince, 'but is he any less ridiculous than the king, or that conceited fellow, or the businessman, or the drunk? At least there is some meaning to his work. When he lights his lamp, it is as if he is giving birth to a new star or a flower. When he puts his light out, that sends the flower or the star off to sleep. That seems to be a rather beautiful profession to have. And because it is beautiful, that makes it truly useful.'

When he came down on the planet, he greeted the lamplighter courteously.

'Good morning to you,' said the little prince. 'Why are you putting out your lamp?'

'I have my orders,' replied the lamplighter, 'and good morning to you.'

'What are your orders exactly?'

'To put out my lamp. Good evening to you.'

And he lit his lamp again.

'So why are you lighting it up again?'

'I have my orders,' the lamplighter told him.

'I don't understand,' said the little prince.

'There's nothing to understand. Orders are orders. That's all there is to it. Good morning to you.' And once again he put out his lamp. Then dabbing his brow with a red check handkerchief, he said: 'It's terribly hard work, you know. It was all right before, in the old days. Every morning I would put out my lamp, and every evening I'd light it up. I had all the rest of each day to put my feet up, and all night to sleep.'

'So your orders must have changed since then, I suppose?' said the little prince.

'No, not at all,' the lamplighter explained. 'That's the whole problem. The problem is that every year the planet is going round faster and faster, but my orders stay just the same.'

'So?' said the little prince.

'So now the planet is making a complete circuit in one minute, and as a result I don't get a second's rest. Once a minute, I have to light my lamp and put it out.'

'Goodness me: how funny! So a day on this planet of yours lasts only one minute.'

It's terribly hard work, you know.

'Actually, it's not funny at all,' said the lamplighter. 'You and I, we have already been talking to one another for an entire month!'

'Really?!'

'Yes. Thirty minutes. Thirty days. Good evening to you.'

And he lit his lamp once again.

As the little prince watched him at work, he found himself liking this lamplighter who was so conscientious about his orders. He remembered how he had to move his chair around to watch the sunsets back at home on his planet. He wanted to help his friend somehow.

'You know,' the little prince began, 'I think I know a way you could rest up whenever you felt like it.'

'The truth is that I always feel like a rest,' said the lamplighter.

Of course it is perfectly possible to be conscientious and lazy at the same time.

The little prince explained his idea: 'Well, your planet is so small that I reckon you could walk all around it in three steps. All you have to do is walk quite slowly, and you would always stay in the sunshine, in daytime. So when you want to rest, you just keep walking, and then the day would last as long as you wanted it to.'

'I'm not sure that would help much,' said the lamplighter. 'What I love most in life is to sleep.'

'Then I'm afraid you're out of luck,' said the little prince.

'It would seem so,' agreed the lamplighter. 'Good morning to you.' And once more he put out his lamp.

Once more on his journey the little prince said to himself: 'My lamplighter friend would be looked down upon by all those others I've met on my travels, by the king, by that conceited fellow, by the drunk, and by the businessman. And yet the lamplighter is the one who does not seem to me to be ridiculous. Maybe that's because he's the only one who thinks about anything else but himself.'

He sighed. Full of regret, he thought to himself: 'He's the only one of them I really wanted to have as a friend. But his planet is far too small, and there's certainly not room enough for two.'

The little prince did not want to admit it to himself, but he was sorrier still about leaving this planet behind him, because every twenty-four hours it was blessed with one thousand four hundred and forty sunsets!

Chapter XV

The sixth planet the little prince happened to visit was ten times the size of the last one. On this planet there lived an old gentleman who wrote great thick books.

'Well I never! An explorer!' exclaimed this old gentleman, on seeing the little prince. The little prince sat himself down at the table. He was completely exhausted, for it had been a long journey.

'Where do you come from?' the old gentleman said to him.

'What is this huge book?' he asked the old gentleman. 'What is it that you do exactly?'

'I am a geographer,' replied the old gentleman.

'What is a geographer?' asked the little prince.

'A geographer is a scholar who knows where to find all the oceans, and rivers, and towns and mountains and deserts.'

'That is so interesting,' said the little prince. 'At last, someone with a proper profession.' He looked around at the geographer's planet. He had never seen a more splendid looking planet than this.

'Your planet,' he went on, 'is so beautiful. Are there any oceans here?'

'Difficult to know,' said the geographer.

'Oh,' said the little prince, who was rather disappointed with this reply. 'And are there any mountains then?' he asked.

'Again, it's difficult to know,' the geographer said.

'And what about towns and rivers and deserts? Have you any of those?'

'Well, that's difficult to know as well,' said the geographer.

'But you are a geographer, so surely … '

'Very true,' the geographer said, 'but I am not an explorer. I have no explorers here on my planet at all. It is not for a geographer like me to go out and actually count the towns and rivers and mountains and oceans and deserts. A geographer is far too important to waste time just wandering about the place. He never leaves his study. He may of course sometimes be visited by explorers. He might question them, and then note down certain accounts of their travels. And if one of these accounts seems to a geographer especially interesting, then the geographer might look into what kind of man the explorer is – his moral code, all that sort of thing.'

'Why would he do that?' asked the little prince.

'Because an explorer who does not tell the truth can cause grave problems for a geographer, problems that could prove catastrophic for his books. And so would an explorer who might prove to be a drunk.'

'Why is that a problem?' asked the little prince.

'Because drunks see double, so the geographer would record two mountains in a place when there was really only one.'

'Then I think I know someone,' the little prince said, 'who would make a really bad explorer.'

'Very likely, I'm sure. And when I am sure the explorer is of good character, then an enquiry is carried out into any discovery he claims to have made.'

'So you go and see for yourself?'

'No, that would be too complicated. But it is important to insist that the explorer shows some proof of his discoveries. So if he says he has discovered a great mountain, it would be necessary for him to bring back some giant rocks from it as evidence.'

The geographer became suddenly very animated. 'But you, you have come from far away, haven't you? And you are an explorer. You must tell me all about your planet.'

And with that, the geographer opened his notebook, and sharpened his pencil. 'The geographer notes down in his book,' he went on, 'everything an explorer tells him. But he only writes it in ink once an explorer has provided proper proof of the truth of his story. Well?' The geographer was waiting expectantly.

'Oh dear,' said the little prince, 'I'm afraid it's not that interesting. My planet is tiny. I have three volcanoes, two of them active, and one extinct. But you never know!'

'That's true,' agreed the geographer.

'And I have one flower as well.'

'We don't record flowers,' said the geographer.

'But why not?' cried the little prince. 'They are so beautiful!'

'We do not record them, because flowers are ephemeral.'

'What does ephemeral mean exactly?'

'You have to understand that books on geography,' said the geographer, 'are the most serious and important of all books. They must never go out of date. Only very rarely does a mountain change where it is. Only very rarely does an ocean dry up. We only write about what lasts, what is eternal.'

'But extinct volcanoes can awaken and become active again,' said the little prince, interrupting him. 'What does ephemeral mean exactly?'

'Whether volcanoes are dormant or active, it's all the same to us,' said the geographer. 'What matters to us is the mountain. A mountain does not change.'

'But what does "ephemeral" mean exactly,' the little prince asked yet again. Once he had asked a question, he never in his life gave up until he received a proper answer.

'It means,' replied the geographer, 'something that is bound sooner or later to disappear.'

'You mean that my flower is bound to disappear?' the little prince exclaimed.

'Of course it is.'

'My dear little flower is ephemeral,' the little prince said to himself. 'And she has only four thorns to defend herself against the world. And I have left her behind at home all alone!'

For the little prince this was a moment of deep regret. But he soon took heart again.

'What planet do you think I should visit next?' he asked the geographer.

'The planet Earth,' replied the geographer. 'I hear it has a good reputation.'

And so the little prince left, still thinking of his flower.

Chapter XVI

So the seventh planet on the little prince's journey was Earth. The Earth is not any old planet! There are one hundred and eleven kings on Earth. There are seven thousand geographers, nine hundred thousand businessmen, seven and a half million drunks, three hundred and eleven million conceited men puffed up with vanity. That's about two billion grown-ups in total.

To give you some idea of the dimensions of Earth I should tell you that before the invention of electricity, it was necessary to employ, on all the six continents of Earth, a veritable army of four hundred and sixty-two thousand, five hundred and eleven lamplighters.

Seen from some distance away they created the most splendid spectacle you can imagine. Their movements were strictly choreographed, just like a ballet.

First on came the lamplighters of New Zealand and Australia. And once their lamps were lit, they went off to bed. Then in their turn came the dance of the lamplighters from China and Siberia, after which they would disappear into the wings. After them it was the turn of the Russian lamplighters and the Indian lamplighters. Then came the African and European lamplighters, and after them those from South America and North America. And they never made any mistakes, always coming on stage at exactly the right moment. It was a magnificent spectacle!

Only the lamplighter in charge of the North Pole, and his colleague responsible for the lamp at the South Pole, led relaxed and easy lives. They had to work just twice a year.

Chapter XVII

When we are trying to be witty, it's fair to say we can find ourselves straying a little from the truth. Now, I have not been entirely honest

The little prince was very surprised to find no one there.

with you about the lamplighters on Earth. In doing so, I might have given a somewhat false idea of Earth to those who are not familiar with the place. The truth is that people occupy very little space on Earth. If all the two billion people who live on the surface of the planet were to stand there, all crowded together as they might be at some great gathering, they would fit easily into a public place about twenty miles long by twenty miles wide. You could cram all of humanity on to the smallest island in the Pacific.

Of course, grown-ups generally don't believe any of this. They imagine they occupy much more space than they do. They see themselves as just as important as the baobabs. Just tell them to do the sums themselves. They love figures and numbers – there is nothing they like better. But don't waste too much time over it. There's no need. Don't worry, you can trust me.

So, once he had landed on Earth, the little prince was very surprised to find no one there. He was becoming worried that he might have come to the wrong planet altogether, when he saw something shining in the sand. It looked like a coil of gold, and was the colour of moonlight.

'Good evening,' he said, just for something to say.

'And good evening to you,' said the snake, for that's what it was.

'Tell me, what planet have I arrived on?' asked the little prince.

'On Earth, in Africa,' the snake replied.

'Really! But is there no one down here on Earth then, no people?'

'This is the desert,' said the snake. 'You will find no people in deserts. But the Earth is a big place.'

The little prince sat down on a stone and looked up at the sky. 'I'm wondering,' he said, 'if the stars light up so that we can all find our own. Look, that's my planet, right there above us. Look how far away it is!'

'It looks beautiful,' said the snake. 'But why have you come here?'

'I have been having a bit of trouble with a flower,' said the little prince.

'I see,' said the snake. And they both fell silent.

'Where are all the people?' the little prince asked after a while. 'I'm beginning to feel lonely in this desert.'

'You can feel lonely in amongst people too,' said the snake.

The little prince looked at the snake for a long time. 'You are a funny-looking creature,' he said, 'as thin as a finger.'

'Maybe, but I assure you I am more powerful than the finger of any king.'

The little prince had to smile at this. 'You're not powerful at all … you haven't even got any feet. You certainly can't travel far, can you?'

'I tell you,' said the snake, 'I could carry you farther than any ship.'

He coiled himself round the little prince's leg like a golden anklet.

'Whoever I touch,' the snake went on, 'I can send back to the earth they came from. But you are an innocent and you come from a star.'

The little prince said nothing.

'I feel sad for you,' the snake said. 'You seem so weak and vulnerable down here on this granite planet, on this inhospitable Earth. One day maybe, I could help you out, if ever you find you are missing your planet too much …'

'Perhaps,' the little prince said. 'But tell me, why do you always speak in riddles?'

'I can solve them all, that's why,' the snake replied.

And they said nothing more.

You are a funny-looking creature . . . as thin as a finger.

Chapter XVIII

The little prince walked on through the desert and met only one flower on the way. It wasn't much of a flower – she had only three petals.

'Good morning,' said the little prince.

'Good morning yourself,' said the flower.

'Where are all the people?' the little prince asked her most politely.

The flower, it seems, just once had seen a caravan passing by. 'People? I think there are only about six or seven of them in existence. I did see some – it was a few years ago now. But they are difficult to find. The wind blows them this way and that. They don't have roots, you see. And that makes life very difficult for them, I think.' And that was that.

'Goodbye,' said the little prince.

'Goodbye yourself,' said the flower.

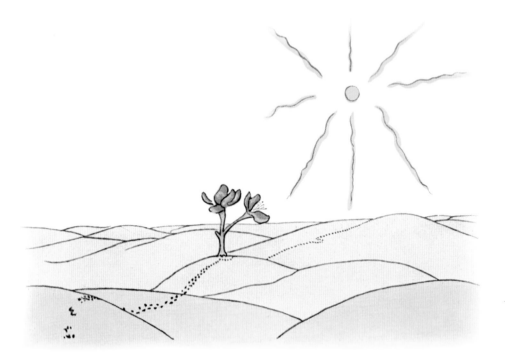

Chapter XIX

The little prince climbed one day right to the summit of a high mountain. The only mountains he had ever known until then were his three volcanoes at home, which were only knee-high. He had used the extinct volcano as a stool to sit on. 'From the summit of a mountain as high as this, surely I will be able to see the entire planet at one glance,' he said to himself, 'and all the people too.'

But all he could see all around him were mountain peaks all as pointed as needles.

'Hello!' he said, just to be polite.

'Hello … hello … hello,' the echo replied.

'Who are you?' asked the little prince.

'Who are you … who are you … who are you,' answered the echo.

'Please be my friends,' the little prince replied. 'I am all alone,' he said.

'I am all alone … all alone … all alone … ' the echo replied.

'What a weird sort of a planet,' thought the little prince. 'Everything is harsh and forbidding and pointed. And as for the people, they clearly have little intelligence and imagination. They just repeat everything you say to them. At home I had my flower, and she was always the one who spoke to me first.'

Everything is harsh and forbidding and pointed.

Chapter XX

It so happened that, after a long trek across the sand, over rocks and through snow, the little prince at last came to a road. And roads lead to people.

He soon found himself walking in a rose garden.

'Hello,' he said.

'Hello to you,' the roses replied.

The little prince gazed at them. Every single one of them looked just like his flower at home. He was amazed.

'Who on earth are you?' he asked them.

'We are roses,' the roses told him.

'I can see that,' the little prince said, but he was feeling very disappointed and upset. Hadn't his flower told him she was the only one of her kind in the entire universe? And here were five thousand of them in one garden, and every one of them the same as his flower back home.

'She would be so cross if ever she saw this,' he thought. 'She would cough and cough and cough, and make believe that she was dying, anything to avoid ridicule and humiliation. And then I would have to pretend to look after her and nurse her back to life. And if I didn't, then, just to put me in my place, she would let herself fade away and die anyway.'

These gloomy thoughts rambled on and on: 'I thought I was rich beyond measure in having a flower that was quite unique, and now I find that I had nothing but a common rose, a plain ordinary rose. And I had three volcanoes that are only big enough to come up to my knees, and one of these is probably extinct for ever. None of this makes me much of a prince, does it?'

And the little prince lay down on the grass and wept.

Chapter XXI

Just then the fox came along.

'Good morning,' said the fox.

'And good morning to you,' replied the little prince, politely. He looked all around, but there was nothing and no one there.

'I am over here,' said the voice. 'Under the apple tree.'

'I see you. Who are you?' asked the little prince. 'You are very beautiful.'

'I'm a fox,' said the fox.

'Won't you come and play with me?' the little prince said. 'I'm so very sad today.'

'I can't play with you,' replied the fox, 'because I have not been tamed.'

'I'm so sorry about that,' said the little prince. But then he thought about it, and added, 'What exactly does "tamed" mean?'

'You're not from around here, are you?' said the fox. 'What is it that you're looking for?'

'I'm looking for people,' the little prince told him. 'But what exactly does "tamed" mean?'

'People have guns and they hunt you,' said the fox, 'which is most inconvenient. They also keep chickens. That's all they seem to want to do, which is fine by me. Are you looking for chickens?'

'No,' said the little prince. 'I'm looking for friends. Please tell me. What exactly does "tamed" mean?'

'Well, it's something too often forgotten,' said the fox. 'I suppose it means: to make some kind of relationship.'

'Relationship?'

'Yes,' said the fox. 'I'll explain. To me, you are just a little boy like any other, like a hundred thousand other little boys. I have no need of you, and you have no need of me. To you I am a fox like any other, like a hundred thousand other foxes. But if you tame me, you and I, we will have created a relationship, and so we will need one another. You will be unique in the world for me.'

'I think I am beginning to understand,' said the little prince. 'There's this flower I know … I think perhaps she tamed me …'

'Quite possibly,' said the fox. 'On Earth you come across all sorts of things.'

'Oh, but this flower is not on Earth,' said the little prince.

The fox seemed really intrigued at this: 'You mean this flower is growing on some other planet?'

'Yes.'

'Are there hunters on this planet?'

'No.'

'Really? That's very interesting indeed. And what about chickens?'

'No. No chickens.'

'Ah well,' the fox sighed. 'Nothing is perfect.'

Then the fox took up his idea again. 'My life is rather tedious,' he went on. 'I hunt chickens. People hunt me. All chickens look alike. All people look alike. I am really so bored with it all. But, if you were to tame me, my whole life would be so much more fun. I would come to know the sound of your footstep, and it would be different from all the others. At the sound of any other footstep I would be down in my hole in the earth as quick as you like. But your footstep would be like music to my ears, and I would come running up out of my hole, as quick as you like.

'And look over there,' the fox went on. 'You see the wheat field? I don't eat bread. Wheat for me is useless. Wheat fields mean nothing to me at all. And that's sad. You have hair the colour of gold. Think just how wonderful it would be if you were to tame me. Wheat, which is gold of course, would always remind me of you. And I would then love the sound of the wind in the wheat.'

The fox, who fell silent now for a while, gazed up at the little prince.

'Please,' said the fox. 'Please tame me.'

'I should like to,' replied the little prince. 'But I don't have much time. I need to find some friends, and there is so much else I have to discover and understand.'

'It's only by taming things that you will ever understand them,' said the fox. 'People never have the time to understand anything that is worthwhile. They buy everything ready made in the shops. That's why people don't have friends, because they can't buy friends in the shops. If you want a friend, then tame me.'

'How would I go about taming you?' asked the little prince.

'Well, you have to be very patient,' the fox replied. 'To start with you have to sit down in the grass a little way away from me – yes, just like that. Then I look at you out of the corner of my eye, and you say nothing. Language is the cause of so many misunderstandings. Then, every day, you come and sit a little closer, and a little closer.'

So the next day the little prince came back again to continue with the taming of the fox.

'It would work a lot better,' said the fox, 'if I knew you were coming back every day at the same time. So if you come, say, at four o'clock in the afternoon, I would begin to relax and be happy at three o'clock. Then, between three o'clock and four o'clock I would begin to feel happier and happier. Otherwise, if I am sitting there waiting for four o'clock to come around, I'll be worrying myself sick. That's what it takes for me to be happy. But if you turn up just when you feel like it, I might well not be in the mood to see you. I am a fox who is a creature of habit, you see.'

'What is habit?' asked the little prince.

'That is also something too often forgotten,' the fox told him. 'Habit is what makes one day different from another, one hour different from another. So for example my hunters, they have their habits. On Thursdays they go dancing with the girls in the village. So Thursdays are always wonderful for me. I can go walking with no worries as far as the vineyards. But if they go dancing whenever they feel like it, every day might be like any other day, and when would a poor old fox like me be able to have his fun?'

The little prince set about taming the fox, but then came the time when he had to leave.

'Oh, dear me,' said the fox, 'I think I am going to cry.'

'Well, it's your fault,' said the little prince. 'I am not blaming you, but you wanted me to tame you.'

'That's true,' said the fox.

'But now you say you're going to cry.'

'Yes,' said the fox.

'So all this taming hasn't done you any good at all, has it?'

'Yes, it has,' the fox replied, 'because I have learnt to love the colour of golden wheat.' Then he added: 'Go again and look at your roses. You

64

So if you come, say, at four o'clock in the afternoon I would begin to relax and be happy at three o'clock.

will realise then that your rose at home is unique. Come to see me again to say goodbye and I will tell you my secret.'

So the little prince went off to see the roses again.

'You are not at all like my rose,' he told them. 'You still mean nothing to me. No one has tamed you and you have tamed no one. You are just like my fox used to be when I first met him. He was a fox just like a hundred thousand other foxes. But I made him my friend, and now he is unique in the whole world.'

At this the roses became very hurt. But the little prince went on. 'You may be beautiful, but you leave me cold. I certainly would not die for you. And it's true, anyone passing by my rose at home might think she looked exactly like you. But even on her own, she is more important to me than all of you put together, and that's because she was the one I watered myself. She is the one I covered with the cloche to protect her from the wind. It was for her that I killed the caterpillars (except for two or three I left to grow into butterflies). I listened to her endless grumbling. I listened to her boasting, and put up with her silences. That's why she is my rose.'

The little prince went to see the fox one last time.

'Goodbye,' he said.

'And goodbye to you,' the fox said. 'Do you want to hear my secret? It is very simple. The important things in life you cannot see with your eyes, only with your heart.'

'The important things in life you cannot see with your eyes, only with your heart.' The little prince repeated it so as to remember it well.

The fox said: 'It is the time you gave to your rose that makes her so important to you.'

'It is the time I gave to my rose ...' said the little prince, so as to remember it well.

'People have forgotten this truth,' the fox said. 'But you must not forget it. You have to be responsible forever for what you have tamed. You are responsible for your rose...'

'I am responsible for my rose...' the little prince repeated, so as never to forget it.

Chapter XXII

'Good morning,' said the little prince.

'And the same to you,' said the signalman.

'What is it that you do?' the little prince asked.

'I process passengers, in groups of a thousand,' said the signalman. 'I arrange the trains to carry them, sometimes this way, sometimes the other.' At that moment the signalman's box began to shake, and an express train came speeding by, roaring like thunder, all lit up from end to end.

'They're in rather a hurry for something,' said the little prince. 'What are they after?'

'Not even the engine-driver knows that,' said the signalman. At that moment a second express train, all lit up from end to end, came thundering by from the other direction.

'Are they coming back already?' asked the little prince

'It's not the same train,' said the signalman. 'That one's going the other way. There's a junction down the line.'

'Is that because they are not happy where they were?' asked the little prince.

'People are never happy where they are,' said the signalman. And just then, a third express train came thundering by, all lit up from end to end.

'So are they chasing after the first lot of passengers?' asked the little prince.

'They are chasing after nothing and no one,' said the signalman. 'They're all asleep in there, or yawning. Only the children will be looking out, their noses pressed up against the windows.'

'Only children care what they are looking for,' said the little prince. 'They spend hours and hours of their time with a rag doll, and it becomes so precious to them, that if you try to take it away from them, they will cry …'

'Then they are more fortunate than they know,' said the signalman.

Chapter XXIII

'Good morning,' said the little prince.

'Good morning,' said the shopkeeper.

His shop sold pills that were guaranteed to take away your thirst, pills you only needed once a week which meant you no longer needed to drink at all.

'But what's the point of selling them?' asked the little prince.

'It saves people time, lots of time,' replied the shopkeeper. 'Experts have worked it all out. People save fifty-three minutes a week!'

'And what do they do with their fifty-three saved minutes?'

'What ever they like.'

'Well,' said the little prince, 'if I had those fifty-three minutes to spend as I wanted, I think I'd go off for a nice walk and find myself a spring of lovely fresh water, and have a good drink...'

Chapter XXIV

It was the eighth day after my plane came down in the desert, and as I listened to the little prince telling the story about the shopkeeper, I found I was drinking my very last drop of water.

'Your memories are fascinating,' I told the little prince, 'but the trouble is that I still have not repaired my plane, and now I have nothing at all left to drink. I'm telling you, it would make me very happy indeed, if I could go off for a nice walk and find myself a spring of lovely fresh water, and have a good drink.'

'My friend the fox … .' the little prince began.

'My dear friend, please no more about the fox.'

'Why not?'

'Because I am about to die of thirst.'

'Well,' he said, clearly not understanding what I meant at all. 'I think it's a very good thing to have a friend, especially if you're going to die. And as for me, I am very grateful to have had a fox for a friend.'

All I could think was this: 'This fellow simply does not realise the danger I am in. He has never been this hungry or this thirsty. A little more of this sun and he will soon find out what it is like.'

He looked at me then, and must have known at once what I was thinking. 'I'm also thirsty,' he said. 'Let's go and find a well.'

I could only shrug wearily as I agreed. I knew it was quite hopeless and absurd to think you could find a well out there in the immensity of the desert. But anyway, off we went.

We trudged on in silence for hours and hours. Night fell, the stars came out. I saw them as if I were in a dream. I was feverish, I think, because I had become so thirsty. The words of the little prince echoed in my mind.

'So you're thirsty as well, are you?' I asked him. But he did not reply. All he said was: 'Water can be really good for the spirits.'

I didn't understand this, but I said no more. I knew well enough by now not to question him too closely. He was tired. He sat down, and I sat down beside him. After some moments of silence, he spoke again. 'All the stars are beautiful, and that's because of just one flower you cannot even see.'

'That's true enough,' I replied, and saying no more I looked out over the waves of sand under the light of the moon.

'The desert is so beautiful,' the little prince said. And it was true. I have always loved the desert. Sitting on a sand dune, there is nothing to see, nothing to hear, and yet the silence out there seems to glow, to radiate.

'What makes the desert so special,' said the little prince,'is that somewhere out there is a well, a well that is hiding from us.'

And to my amazement, I suddenly understood this mysterious silence of the desert. When I was a small boy, I used to live in an old house. There were stories of buried treasure in this house. Of course, no one had ever found any, nor had anyone probably even looked for it. But that story brought a mysterious enchantment to that whole house. My house was hiding a secret deep in its heart.

'Yes,' I said to the little prince, 'whether we are thinking of a house, or the stars, or the desert, what makes them beautiful is always invisible.'

'I'm so pleased,' said the little prince, 'that you agree with my fox.'

Once the little prince fell asleep, I picked him up in my arms and set off on my way again. I was so moved as I walked. It seemed to me I was carrying in my arms the most delicate of treasures, that there could be nothing more fragile on the whole Earth. In the light of the moon I looked down at this pale forehead, those closed eyes, those locks of his that trembled in the wind: 'What I am seeing,' I thought, 'is no more than the shell. What is truly important I cannot see.'

His lips were open, just slightly, as if half smiling. 'What moves me most about this little prince asleep in my arms is his love and loyalty for a flower. And it is the rose in him that radiates like lamplight, even when he sleeps.' He seemed to me at that moment more delicate and precious than ever. Lamplight has to be protected. One gust of wind is all it takes to blow it out.

I walked on, until at dawn I came upon a well.

Chapter XXV

'People', said the little prince, 'they roar along in express trains, without ever knowing what they are looking for. They rush about, go round and round in circles, and none of it's worth the trouble.'

The well we had arrived at did not look much like a well you might find in the deserts of the Sahara. Wells in the Sahara are no more than holes in the sand. This one was more like a village well. But there was no village. I thought I must be dreaming.

'This is really odd,' I said to the little prince. 'Look, everything is ready and waiting for us: the pulley, the bucket, the rope.'

He laughed, grabbed the rope and began to pull. The pulley groaned like an old weathervane that had long since been forgotten by the wind.

'Do you hear that?' said the little prince. 'We are waking up this well. He is singing to us.'

I did not want him to have to do the pulling and tire himself. 'Let me do it,' I told him. 'It's too heavy for you.'

Slowly, slowly, I hoisted the bucket up to the top of the well, and there I set it down, carefully balancing it on the edge. It was heavy, and I was exhausted, but I was also rather pleased with myself. The song of the pulley echoed on in my ears, and I could see sunlight shimmering on the water and the water still trembling.

'I'm dying for that water,' said the little prince. 'I need a drink, right now.' I knew what he meant.

I lifted the bucket to his lips. He drank, his eyes closed. Then I drank. It was like a feast of water. This was not ordinary food of course, but it might just as well have been.

The sweetness of this water was born from the long walk under the stars, from the song of the pulley, and from the effort of pulling up that bucket. It made me feel good, made me happy, as a present does. When I was a little boy, the Christmas tree lights, the music at Midnight Mass, the sweet smiles all around me – they shone light and warmth on any Christmas present I was given. It was like that.

He laughed, touched the rope and began to pull.

'People here on Earth where you live,' said the little prince, 'might grow five thousand roses in the same garden, and yet they cannot find what they are looking for.'

'You're right,' I replied. 'They never find it.'

'And yet it can be found in one single rose or in a drink of water.'

'That is true,' I said.

'Eyes are blind,' the little prince went on. 'To see things as they are, you have to use your heart.'

I had drunk my fill. I was breathing more easily now. At sunrise, sand is the colour of honey. The sight of it filled me with happiness. So why was I feeling sad at heart?

'You have to keep your promise you know,' said the little prince who spoke quietly to me, as he sat down beside me.

'What promise do you mean?'

'You know, the muzzle for my sheep. I am responsible for that flower of mine.'

I took out my sketchbook. The little prince looked through my drawings, and laughed out loud.

'Your baobabs, they look a little like cabbages to me.'

'Cabbages!' I was rather proud of my baobab drawings.

'And as for your fox, his ears ... they look like horns. They're far too long.'

And he laughed again.

'That's not fair, my dear fellow,' I said. 'I can only really draw boa constrictors – boa constrictors from the inside, or from the outside.'

'Don't worry,' he said, 'children understand these things.'

So I drew a muzzle for him, but as I was handing it over, a deep sense of foreboding came over me, like a shadow. 'Have you got plans you're not telling me about?' I asked him. But there was nothing in reply.

'Tomorrow,' he said, 'will be the anniversary of my arrival on Earth.'

Then after a moment of silence, he went on: 'I landed quite close to here.'

He flushed suddenly, as if he was hiding something. And once more, without understanding why, I felt overwhelmed by sorrow and this was when a sudden thought came to mind. 'So it wasn't just by chance, that on the morning I first met you – a week ago now – I found you wandering about all alone, a thousand miles from any human habitation. You were on your way back to the very place where you first landed on Earth, weren't you?' Now the little prince was looking even more flushed.

I was unsure for a moment whether to go on. 'Was it perhaps,' I said, 'because of the anniversary?'

The little prince flushed again with embarrassment. He never answered questions directly, of course, but when people flush like this, it usually means yes.

'I'm afraid I have upset you…' I began.

But he interrupted me. 'You must get on with your work,' he said. 'You had best get back to your engine. I will wait here for you. Come back tomorrow evening … '

This did not set my mind at rest at all. I remembered the fox. If you allow yourself to be tamed, there will be tears.

Chapter XXVI

Right beside the well there were the ruins of an old stone wall. When I came back from my work on the engine the next evening, I saw my little prince from far away. He was sitting high up there on the wall, his legs dangling. I could hear him talking to someone. 'You don't remember then,' he was saying. 'So it wasn't here at all.' Another voice I couldn't hear must have replied, because the little prince was answering it. 'Yes, yes. I know it's the right day, but this is not the right place.'

As I came closer to the wall, I could not see or hear anyone else. Yet the little prince was answering someone yet again. 'All right. You will see where my tracks begin in the sand. All you have to do is follow them, and then wait for me there. I will be there tonight.'

By this time I was twenty metres from the wall and still I could see no one.

After a few moments of silence, the little prince spoke again. 'Is your venom good? Are you sure it won't make me suffer for too long?'

I stopped where I was, my heart in my mouth. I still could not fully grasp what was going on.

'Now, just go away will you?' said the little prince. 'I want to get down off this wall.'

That was when I spotted something, at the foot of the wall, something that made me start back in terror. There, with his eyes fixed on the little prince, was one of those yellow snakes that can kill you in thirty seconds. I was groping in my pocket for my revolver as I backed away. I began to run, but I must have made too much noise, because the snake slipped into the sand, flowed away like a stream of dying water; seemingly in no hurry at all, disappearing between the stones, with just hint of sounds, almost metallic.

I reached the wall just in time to catch my little prince in my arms. He was as pale as a sheet.

'What does this mean?' I cried. 'Why are you talking to snakes?'

I was taking off the golden scarf he always wore, cooling his temples with water, making him drink. But I didn't dare ask him any more questions. He looked up at me, his eyes full of sorrow, and then wrapped his arms around my neck. I felt the beating of his heart. It was like the heart of a dying bird that had been shot.

'I am so pleased you have found what was wrong with your engine,' he said. 'Now you will be able to go back home.'

'But how did you know?' I asked. It was what I had come for, to break the good news to him that, against all expectations, I had indeed managed to repair my engine.

He did not say a word in reply to my question.

'Me too,' he said. 'I am going home today as well.' Then more sadly, he went on: 'It is a long long way that I am going .... It will be a difficult journey ... very difficult.'

Now, just go away, will you . . . I want to get down off this wall.

I knew that something quite extraordinary was happening. I was holding him in my arms like a little child, for it seemed to me that he was drifting away from me and falling down, down into an abyss, and that there was nothing I could do to save him.

He looked already like someone lost and far away. 'I have your sheep,' he said, 'and I have his box too, and the muzzle.' He smiled sadly. I waited a while, holding him, and he began to revive, to feel better, little by little.

'My dear little fellow,' I said, 'you must have been so frightened.' And he certainly had been terrified. But he just laughed softly, and said:

'I think I shall be much more frightened this evening.'

And again I felt a chill come over me, at the thought that there was nothing more to be done. And I knew I could not bear the idea that I would never hear the sound of his laughter again. For me it was like a spring of fresh water in the desert.

'Dear little fellow,' I said. 'I should love to hear you laugh again.'

But all he said was: 'Tonight, it will be one year … And my star will be right above the place where I came down to Earth this time last year.'

'Dear little fellow, please tell me this whole thing is all just a bad dream, this story of the star and your meeting with the snake? It's not true, is it?'

But he didn't reply to my question.

Instead, he said: 'What's truly important is always what you cannot see …'

'I know that …'

'It's the same with the flower. If you love a flower growing on a star, it is wonderful at night, to gaze up at the sky. Then all the stars will be aglow with flowers.'

'They are, they are.'

'It is the same with water. The water you gave me to drink was like music, because of the pulley and the rope, you remember? It was so good.'

'It was, it was.'

'At night times you will gaze up at the stars,' said the little prince. 'Where I live is too small for me even to show you where you will find my star. It is better that way. My star for you will be just one of the stars up there. Think of it like this, and you will love to look up and wonder at all the stars. They will all be your friends. And now, I am going to give you a present.'

And he laughed again.

'Oh, my dear little fellow my dear little prince, how I love to hear that laugh of yours.'

'And that's my present to you. It will be just like it was when we drank the water.'

'What do you mean?'

'Stars mean different things to different people. For travellers, stars tell them where they are, where they are going. For others, they are just little lights in the sky. For scholars, they are the world of the unknown, yet to be discovered and understood. For my businessman they are gold. But all stars stay silent. And you? No one else in the world will see the stars as you do.'

'I don't understand exactly?'

'When you look up at the sky at night, because I live in one of them, because I will be laughing in one of them, for you it will be as if all the stars are laughing. For you, and only for you, the stars will always be laughing.'

And the little prince was laughing again.

'And once you have got over the sadness of parting (and in time we always do) you will be happy that you knew me. You will always be my friend. You will always want to laugh with me. Sometimes you will open your window, just for the pure pleasure of it, and look out. And when you do, all your friends will be so astonished to see you looking up at the sky, and laughing. You'll say: "Stars, you know, they always make me laugh." They'll think you're quite mad. And you will think I have played a mean sort of a trick on you.' And he laughed again. 'It'll be as if I'd given you, instead of the stars, thousands of little bells up there, all ringing with their laughter.' He laughed and laughed, but then suddenly turned very solemn. 'Tonight, I think it will be better if you don't come.'

'I won't leave you,' I said.

'I will look as if I am suffering,' said the little prince. 'I may even look as if I am dying. It is how it will be. Don't come to see that. It's not worth it.'

'I don't want to leave you,' I said.

He looked suddenly worried. 'I am telling you not to come also because of the snake. I don't want him to bite you. They are nasty, vicious creatures. They can bite just for the fun of it.'

'I tell you I am not going to leave you alone,' I said.

'Of course,' he began, more reassured now. 'Of course it is true that they don't have much venom left for a second bite.'

That night I did not see him leave. The little prince slipped off so silently that I never knew anything. When I finally caught up with him he was walking fast, striding out.

'Ah, there you are.' It was all he said. When he took me by the hand. I could feel he was still deeply troubled. 'You were wrong to come. You will be grieving. I will look as if I am dead, and it will not be true.'

I could not say anything. 'You understand … . It is too far. I can't take this body of mine with me. It is too heavy.'

Still I said nothing.

'It will be like an old empty shell left lying there on the ground. There's nothing sad about an old shell.'

What could I say?

He was losing heart, but he went on anyway. 'It will be all right, you know. I shall look up at the stars too. All the stars will be wells with a rusty pulley. So all the stars will pour out their fresh water for me to drink.'

I said nothing.

'It will be such fun. You will have five hundred million bells, and I will have five hundred million wells.'

Now he too said no more because he was crying.

'We are almost there,' he said. 'I'll go on alone now.'

But then he sat down. I could see he was frightened.

'My flower, I am responsible for her, you know,' he said. 'And she is so fragile, and innocent. She has only four thorns, that's all, to protect herself against the world.'

I sat down nearby. I could no longer stand up.

'Well,' the little prince said, 'I suppose the time has come ...'

For a moment or two, he waited. Then he stood up, and began to walk away. I could not move. It was no more than a flash of yellow close to his ankle. For a moment he stood quite still. He did not cry out. He fell slowly, as a tree falls. There was no sound at all, because he fell on sand.

He fell slowly, as a tree falls. There was no sound at all, because he fell on sand.

Chapter XXVII

It has been six years now, and I have never before this told my story. Friends who saw me afterwards were delighted to see me alive. I must have seemed rather sad. 'I am just tired,' I told them.

Now, I am a little bit happier, or perhaps a little less sad. But I do know for sure that the little prince went back to his planet, because when daylight came, I could not find his body. So it wasn't such a heavy body after all. And I love to go out at night and listen to the stars. They do ring, like five hundred million bells.

But there is something else that occurred to me that I must tell you. I remembered that on the muzzle I drew for the little prince, I forgot to draw a leather strap. Without a strap there was of course no way to keep the muzzle on. So now I keep wondering what is happening up there on his planet. Might the sheep have eaten the flower?

But I tell myself: 'No, surely not. Every night the little prince covers his flower under his glass cloche and he always keeps a watchful eye on his sheep.' Then I am happy enough. And the stars laugh so sweetly up there above me.

But then I keep thinking: 'How easy it is to become distracted from time to time – that's all it would take. Maybe, one evening, he will forget to cover his flower with the cloche, and maybe the sheep will steal away silently in the middle of the night.' Then all the bells up there would turn to tears.

It is all a great mystery, isn't it? For you who love the little prince as I do, nothing in the universe makes any sense at all, unless somewhere – and who knows where? – some unseen sheep has, or has not, eaten a rose.

Look up at the sky. Ask yourself: 'Is it yes or no? Has the sheep eaten the flower, yes or no?' Do it, and you will see how everything changes.

And no grown-up will ever understand just how important that is.

This for me is the most beautiful and the saddest landscape in the whole world. It's the same as the one on the opposite page. I have drawn it once more just so you don't forget it. This is where the little prince appeared on Earth, and then disappeared.

Look carefully, so that you will recognise it if ever your travels take you one day to the deserts of Africa. And if you do happen to pass that way, don't hurry on by, but instead wait for a while right under the star. And if a little fellow comes along, if he laughs, if he has golden hair, and if he never answers questions, then you will know who he is.

If that happens, please be good enough to write to me at once. It would be of such comfort to me to know that he has come back.

VINTAGE CLASSICS

Vintage launched in the United Kingdom in 1990, and was originally the paperback home for the Random House Group's literary authors. Now, Vintage is comprised of some of London's oldest and most prestigious literary houses, including Chatto & Windus (1855), Hogarth (1917), Jonathan Cape (1921) and Secker & Warburg (1935), alongside the newer or relaunched hardback and paperback imprints: The Bodley Head, Harvill Secker, Yellow Jersey, Square Peg, Vintage Paperbacks and Vintage Classics.

From Angela Carter, Graham Greene and Aldous Huxley to Toni Morrison, Haruki Murakami and Virginia Woolf, Vintage Classics is renowned for publishing some of the greatest writers and thinkers from around the world and across the ages – all complemented by our beautiful, stylish approach to design. Vintage Classics' authors have won many of the world's most revered literary prizes, including the Nobel, the Man Booker, the Prix Goncourt and the Pulitzer, and through their writing they continue to capture imaginations, inspire new perspectives and incite curiosity.

In 2007 Vintage Classics introduced its distinctive red spine design, and in 2012 Vintage Children's Classics was launched to include the much-loved authors of our childhood. Random House joined forces with the Penguin Group in 2013 to become Penguin Random House, making it the largest trade publisher in the United Kingdom.

@vintagebooks

penguin.co.uk/vintage-classics